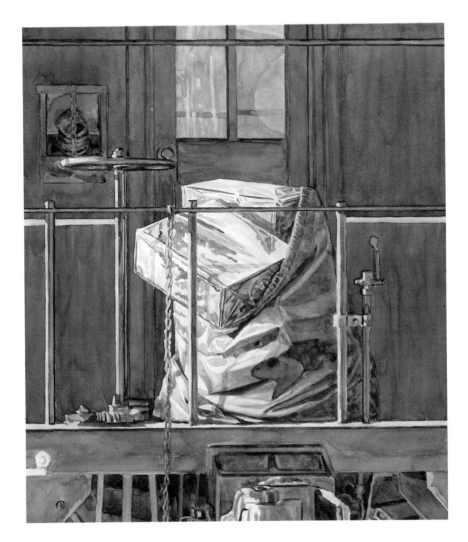

SILVER PACKAGES

A RICHARD JACKSON BOOK

To Tom Bernagozzi and his young writers
—C.R.
To my Korean and adopted families
with thanks for all your support,
and to my wife, Rosanna
—C.K.S.

This story was inspired by a real train, the "Santa Train," which rolls through the Appalachian Mountains each Christmas season. From this train, tons of toys and treats are tossed by volunteers to the children of coal towns who wait patiently by the tracks. This has been happening every Christmas since 1943.—C.R.

Text copyright © 1987 by Cynthia Rylant. Illustrations copyright © 1997 by Chris K. Soentpiet. "Silver Packages" was first published in 1987 in the collection *Children of Christmas: Stories for the Season* by Cynthia Rylant, illustrated by S. D. Schindler. All rights reserved. No part of this book may be reproduced or transmitted in any form or by any means, electronic or mechanical, including photocopying, recording, or by any information storage or retrieval system, without permission in writing from the Publisher. Orchard Books, 95 Madison Avenue, New York, NY 10016. Manufactured in the United States of America Printed by Barton Press, Inc. Bound by Horowitz/Rae. The text of this book is set in 14 point Galliard. The illustrations are watercolor paintings reproduced in full color. Library of Congress Cataloging-in-Publication Data. Rylant, Cynthia. Silver packages : an Appalachian Christmas story / by Cynthia Rylant ; paintings by Chris K. Soentpiet. p.   cm. "A Richard Jackson book"—Half t.p. Summary: Every year at Christmas a rich man rides a train through Appalachia and throws gifts to the poor children who are waiting, in order to repay a debt he owes the people who live there. ISBN 0-531-30051-X. — ISBN 0-531-33051-6 (lib. bdg.) [1. Appalachian Region—Fiction. 2. Christmas—Fiction.   3. Railroads—Trains—Fiction.]   I. Soentpiet, Chris K., ill.   II. Title.   PZ7.R982Si   1997   [E]—dc21   96-53876

10   9 8 7 6 5 4 3 2

SILVER PACKAGES

AN APPALACHIAN CHRISTMAS STORY

by Cynthia Rylant
paintings by Chris K. Soentpiet

ORCHARD BOOKS
NEW YORK

A TRAIN comes through Appalachia every year at Christmas time. And though it doesn't have antlers, nor does the man standing on its rear platform have a long white beard, it may as well be Santa Claus and his sleigh for all the excitement it stirs up.

People call it the Christmas Train. And it has been coming to them for years. Each new child born in the mountains learns to walk, talk, and wait for the Christmas Train.

It is everyone's delight.

The older people remember its beginning. They tell of a rich man who had come traveling through the hills by car many years back. No one knows why he came up into the hills, but why isn't important. What matters is what happened.

The man had an accident. His car just took itself right over the side of a ridge, and the man slumped in that car, hurting and scared. Someone came along. Some say it was old Mr. Crookshank, but others say it was Betty Pritt. But who came along isn't important either.

Whoever it was pulled that rich man out of his car and took him to a house in the hills where he was nursed and cared for until he could make it out on his own. When he left, the rich man tried to give money to the people who had helped him. But they would not accept it.

So that rich man left the mountains feeling he owed a great debt. And for the remaining years of his life, he has been repaying this debt from the caboose of a Christmas Train he brings into the hills each December.

On the twenty-third—everybody knows it—the train will slowly wind up and around the mountains, and on the platform of its caboose will stand the rich man in a blue wool coat. He will toss a sparkling silver package into the hands of each child who waits beside the tracks, and for some, it will be the only present they receive.

So the train is awfully important.

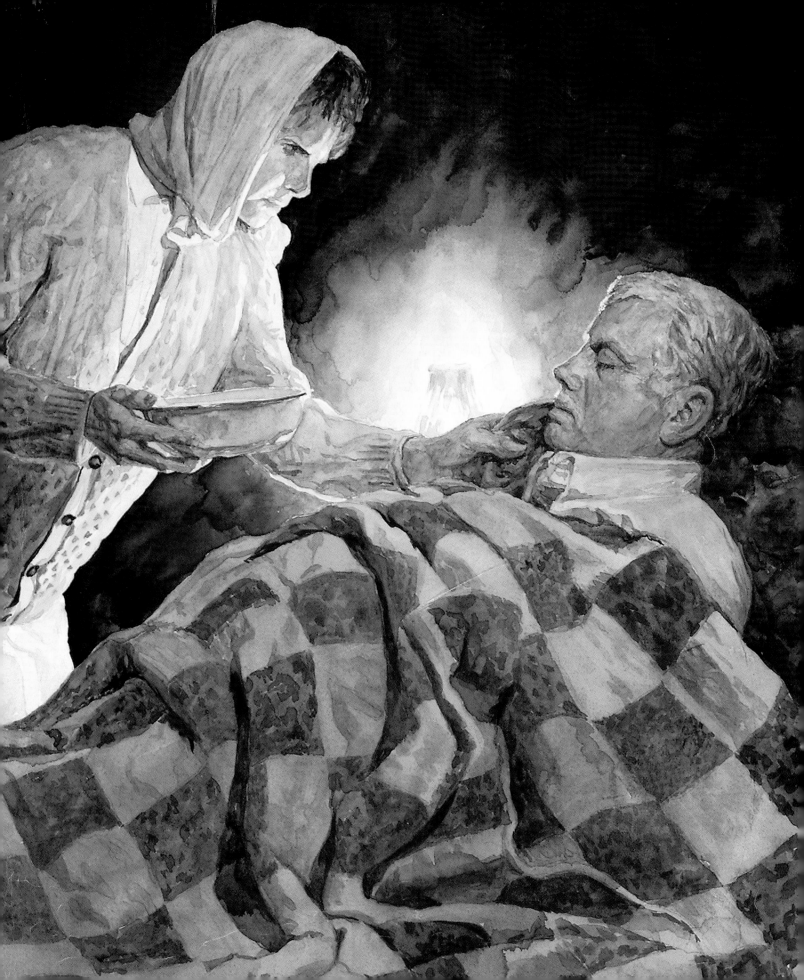

One year a boy named Frankie stands beside those tracks and waits for the Christmas Train. It is very cold and a lot of snow has come down the night before. Frankie's shoes are thin and his feet hurt badly from the cold. But he is determined to wait, even if his feet and all the rest of him become ice.

Now this particular boy wants a particular present. Not just any present tossed from the back of that train. A *particular* present: a doctor kit. He's been waiting for it, beside the tracks.

The train comes through finally. Noisy and steaming and scary, it is so big, but everyone loves to see it and they cheer and clap and some of the mothers even weep to see it coming.

Frankie stands there at the tracks, praying for a doctor kit, till he sees the caboose slowly coming up. And when it is just past his nose, he shouts and waves and runs after the train, his icy feet aching.

From the rear platform, the rich man in the wool coat sees him.
"Merry Christmas!" he calls.
And he tosses into Frankie's hands a sparkling silver package.
Frankie stops running. He is out of breath, so he can't yell a thank-you. He can only hold tight to his gift and wave to the man and the train disappearing into the mountains.

Frankie carries his package home, and puts his own name on it, and sets it under the family Christmas tree. On Christmas morning, he opens it.

It isn't a doctor kit. It's a cowboy holster set and three pairs of thick red socks.

Frankie looks at his mother and father and brothers and sisters and tries not to cry.

He wears the socks all winter and plays with the cowboy set all
year. But he dreams of a doctor kit.

The next Christmas Frankie waits again in the cold for the
Christmas Train. The socks still fit him, so his feet are warm. But his
fingers are cold and hurting.

He waits at the tracks and prays for a doctor kit. The train comes;
the rich man tosses the silver package.

And on Christmas morning, Frankie opens it.

No.

It is a little police car with lights that really work plus two pairs of brown mittens.

Frankie doesn't cry.

He wears the mittens all winter and plays with the car all year. But he dreams of a doctor kit.

Frankie waits three more years for a doctor kit. It never comes. He gets trucks and balls and games. He gets mittens and socks and hats and scarves.

But the doctor kit never comes.

When Frankie grows up, he moves away, out of the hills. He lives in different places and meets different kinds of people and he himself changes a little into a different kind of person.

But deep in him, never changing, are his memories. And what he remembers most about being a boy in the hills is that just when it seemed his feet would freeze like the snow, a man on a train had brought socks. Just when it seemed his fingers were hardening to ice, the man had brought mittens. Just when the cold wind was cutting sharp as a blade into his throat, the man had brought a scarf. And just when Frankie's ears were numb with red cold, the man had brought a hat.

And Frankie remembers something about owing a debt.

So, a grown man who has been gone a long time moves back into those same mountains to live. His brothers and sisters are still there, waiting for him.

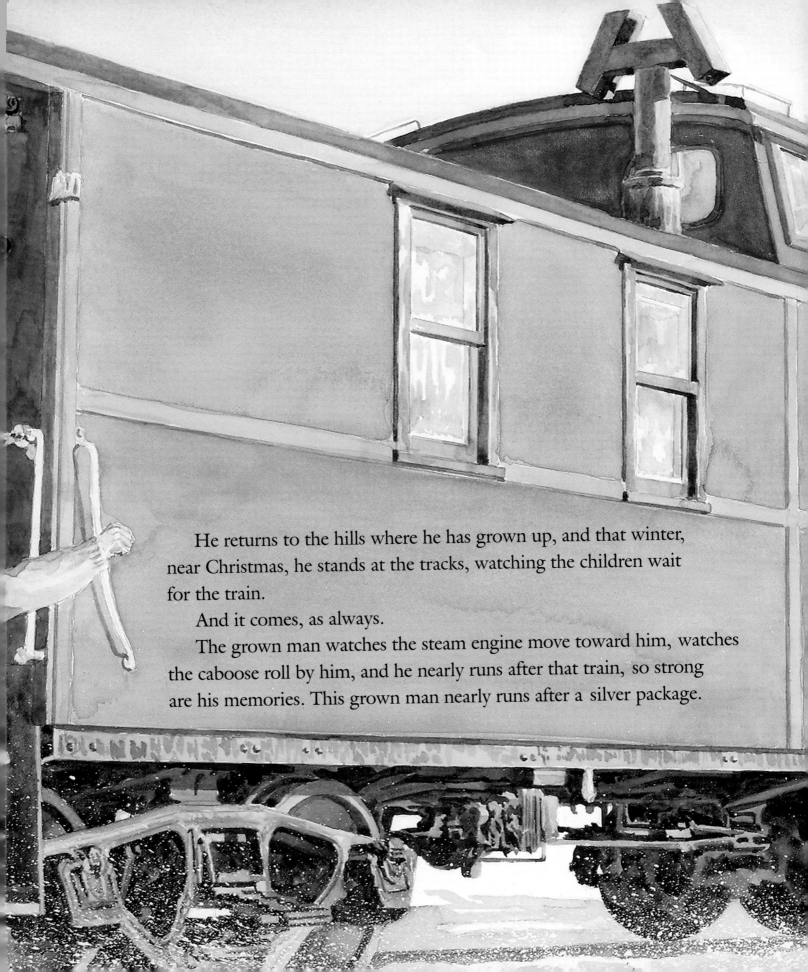

He returns to the hills where he has grown up, and that winter, near Christmas, he stands at the tracks, watching the children wait for the train.

And it comes, as always.

The grown man watches the steam engine move toward him, watches the caboose roll by him, and he nearly runs after that train, so strong are his memories. This grown man nearly runs after a silver package.

But instead he watches a little girl chase that caboose, watches a
man in a wool coat toss her a sparkling silver package, watches the gift
land near the little girl's feet, watches her running so fast that she trips
on her silver package, watches her fall hard to the ground.

The grown man does run now, but not for a train. Not for a rich
man in a wool coat. For a little girl.

He picks her up. He wipes away her tears with the scarf from around his neck. He smiles at her.

"It's okay, little one," he says easily. The train is disappearing into the trees. He had meant to wave to the rich man. But there wasn't time.

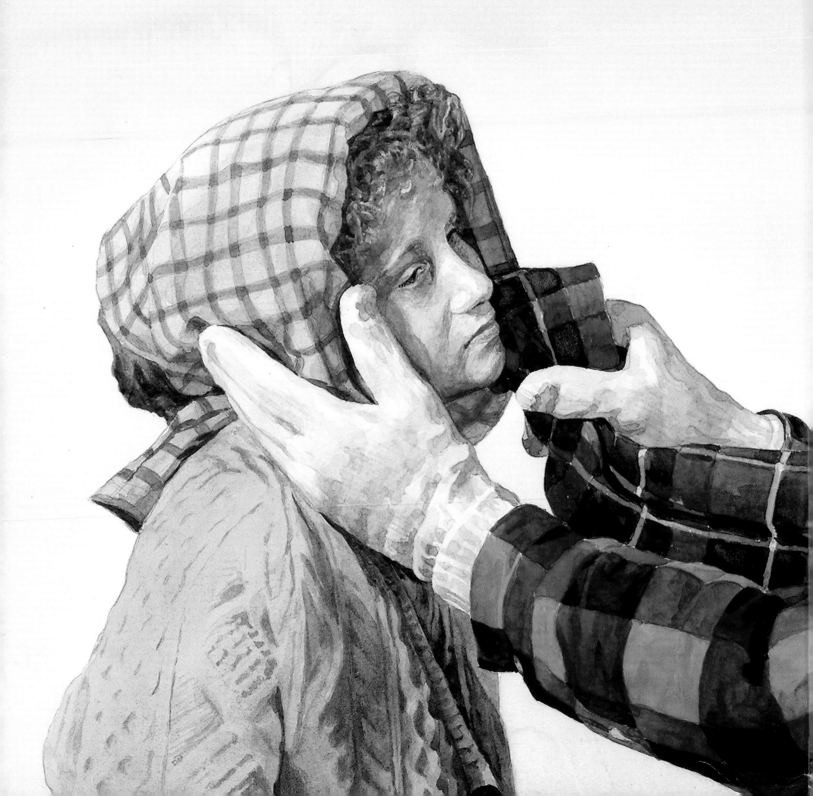

He picks up the silver package and puts it into the little girl's arms.
"You'll be all right," he tells her. "I'll make sure."
He pulls open his kit to look for a Band-Aid.
"Name's Frank." He smiles. "I'm a doctor."